HELLO, I'M THEA!

I'm *Geronimo Stilton*'s sister. As I'm sure you know from my brother's bestselling novels, I'm a special correspondent for *The Rodent's Gazette*, Mouse Island's most famous newspaper. Unlike my 'fraidy mouse brother, I absolutely adore traveling, having adventures, and meeting rodents from all around the world!

The adventure I want to tell you about begins at Mouseford Academy, the school I went to when I was a young mouseling. I had such a great experience there as a student that I came back to teach a journalism class.

When I returned as a grown mouse, I met five really special students: Colette, Nicky, Pamela, Paulina, and Violet. You could hardly imagine five more different mouselings, but they became great friends right away. And they liked me so much that they decided to name their group after me: the Thea Sisters! I was so touched by that, I decided to write about their adventures. So turn the page to read a fabumouse adventure about the

THEA SISTERS!

Nicky

Name: Nicky

Nickname: Nic

Home: Australia

Secret ambition: Wants to be an ecologist.

Loves: Open spaces and nature.

Strengths: She is always in a good mood, as long as she's outdoors!

Weaknesses: She can't sit still!

Secret: Nicky is claustrophobic — she can't stand being in small, tight places.

Nicky

COLETTE

Name: Colette

Nickname: It's Colette, please. (She can't stand nicknames.)

Home: France

Secret ambition: Colette is very particular about her appearance. She wants to be a fashion writer.

Loves: The color pink.

Strengths: She's energetic and full of great ideas.

Weaknesses: She's always late!

Secret: To relax, there's nothing Colette likes more than a manicure and pedicure.

Colette

VIOLET

Name: Violet
Nickname: Vi
Home: China
Secret ambition: Wants to become a great violinist.
Loves: Books! She is a real intellectual, just like my brother, Geronimo.
Strengths: She's detail-oriented and always open to new things.
Weaknesses: She is a bit sensitive and can't stand being teased. And if she doesn't get enough sleep, she can be a real grouch!
Secret: She likes to unwind by listening to classical music and drinking green tea.

Violet

Name: Paulina
Nickname: Polly
Home: Peru
Secret ambition: Wants to be a scientist.
Loves: Traveling and meeting people from all over the world. She is also very close to her sister, Maria.
Strengths: Loves helping other rodents.
Weaknesses: She's shy and can be a bit clumsy.
Secret: She is a computer genius!

PAULINA

PAULINA

Name: Pamela
Nickname: Pam
Home: Tanzania

PAMELA

Secret ambition: Wants to become a sports journalist or a car mechanic.

Loves: Pizza, pizza, and more pizza! She'd eat pizza for breakfast if she could.

Strengths: She is a peacemaker. She can't stand arguments.

Weaknesses: She is very impulsive.

Secret: Give her a screwdriver and any mechanical problem will be solved!

Pamela

Geronimo Stilton

Thea Stilton
AND THE GHOST
OF THE SHIPWRECK

Scholastic Inc.

New York   Toronto   London   Auckland
Sydney   Mexico City   New Delhi   Hong Kong

ISBN: 978-0-545-15059-0

Copyright © 2007 by Edizioni Piemme S.p.A., Via Galeotto del Carretto 10, 15033 Casale Monferrato (AL), Italy. International Rights @ Atlantyca S.p.A., Via Telesio 22, 20145 Milan, Italy, *foreignrights@atlantyca.it*

English translation © 2010 by Atlantyca S.p.A.

Text by Thea Stilton
Based on an original idea by Elisabetta Dami
Original title *Il Vascello Fantasma*
Cover by Arianna Rea, Paolo Ferrante, and Ketty Formaggio
Illustrations by Maria Abagnale, Alessandro Battan, Fabio Bono, Jacopo Brandi, Paolo Ferrante, Claudia Forcelloni, Daniela Geremia, Marco Meloni, Roberta Pierpaoli, and Arianna Rea
Color by Giulia Basile, Fabio Bonechi, Alessandro Bracaglia, Ketty Formaggio, Daniela Geremia, Donatella Melchionno, and Micaela Tangorra
Graphics by Paola Cantoni
Special thanks to Beth Dunfey and Julia Heim
Interior design by Kay Petronio

12 11 10 9 8 7 6 5 4 3   10 11 12 13 14 15/0

Printed in the U.S.A.   40
First printing, March 2010

SURPRISE!!!

This year, summer came early to New Mouse City. By noontime, the **sun** was so hot, the **STREETS** started baking. But at sunrise, when that delicious *little breeze* blew in from the east, it was wonderful to scamper through the park!

That was my **favorite** time of day, before I went to work at *The Rodent's Gazette*. You know about *The Rodent's Gazette*, right? It's the famouse newspaper run by my brother, *Geronimo Stilton!*

One day, I had just

Thea Stilton

Help the members of the Thea Sisters solve the mystery! When you see this magnifying glass, pay attention: It means there's an important clue on that page.

returned from my morning JOG when my intercom buzzed.

"Hello? Who is it?" I asked, peeking at the teeny screen.

"Surprise!!!" five smiling snouts squeaked in unison.

"Holey cheese!" I shrieked in delight. "Come on up, mouselings!"

I threw open the door and scurried out to meet my dear friends — the Thea Sisters. They were five young mouselings I had met while teaching a course in adventure journalism at my alma mater, Mouseford Academy, on Whale Island. I couldn't wait to put my paws around my five friends!

"Colette! Nicky! Pamela!

PAULINA! **Violet!**" I hugged them all at once. What *joy* to see them all again! "Why aren't you at **MOUSEFORD ACADEMY**? What brings you to New Mouse City?"

"A new adventure," Pam announced **MYSTERIOUSLY**.

"And we got a free ferry ride from Vince Guymouse!" added Paulina, enjoying my look of **ASTONISHMENT**.

Violet came to my rescue. "Don't confuse her, mouselings! Tell her everything while I go make us some tea."

We all sat down, and as the Thea Sisters took turns squeaking, I quickly realized that I had found a new and exciting **ADVENTURE** to write about.

It all started on Whale Island, immediately after Mouseford Academy's SPRING break. . . .

THE SMELL OF
SWEET CHEESE

Spring break had just ended, and students were returning to Mouseford Academy. The campus paths were dotted with brightly COLORED T-shirts and backpacks as the students scurried around, greeting one another eagerly.

Professor Octavius de Mousus, the headmaster, stood at the academy's main entrance.

He noticed some mouselings **gathering** in a corner of the campus garden. What was going on down there?

Just then, Colette scampered up to him, a BIG SMILE on her snout. "Hi, Professor! Would you like to join us in the

garden? We're having a little snack of special Australian cheeses! We've just returned from visiting Nicky at her family's sheep ranch."

Professor de Mousus followed Colette into the garden, where there was a table covered in food. The students and teachers were mingling, chatting, and snacking.

"These cheddar crackers are delicious!"

"Did you try the feta Nicky's grandmother made?"

"MMM . . . it's amazing!"

Colette, Nicky, Pamela, and Paulina were busy telling all their friends about their recent adventures in Australia. The only one who was off by herself was Violet. She was chewing on a **CHEESE STICK** and checking her watch. Finally, she whispered to Paulina, "I'm going to save some seats in the auditorium."

"But why?" asked Paulina. "**Professor Ian van Kraken**'s lecture doesn't start until eleven!"

Violet **blushed** and *HURRIED* away.

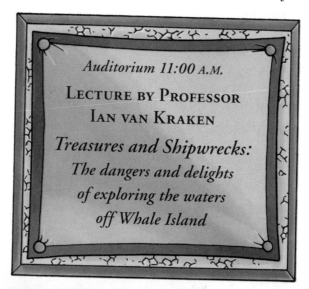

Auditorium 11:00 A.M.

LECTURE BY PROFESSOR IAN VAN KRAKEN

Treasures and Shipwrecks:
The dangers and delights
of exploring the waters
off Whale Island

JASMINE'S HEART

Professor Ian van Kraken was responsible for **TIDE HOUSE**, the marine biology laboratory that was an unofficial part of **MOUSEFORD ACADEMY**. Students loved attending his lectures. He was a fascinating squeaker.

When Colette, Nicky, Pamela, and Paulina arrived, the auditorium was full, but Violet had saved four seats in the front row.

"Thanks, Vi!" said Nicky, slipping into the seat next to her.

Colette winked at Violet. She suspected her quiet friend had a spot as soft as Brie for their professor. "How long have you been waiting? Have you started growing roots?"

Violet didn't seem to hear her. She was

completely focused on the **BRIGHT** blue **EYES** of Professor van Kraken, who was striding onstage. He was a tall, handsome mouse with a *tuft* of blond fur. His one true *love* was the **sea**.

Professor Ian van Kraken

"Today I'm going to talk to you about one of **WHALE ISLAND**'s most famouse legends," the professor began. "One day, toward the beginning of the sixteenth century, a terrible **storm** broke out in the waters off the island's western coast. A galleon named the Queen Mousy was heading toward **INDIA**. Marius von Opul was on board, carrying a priceless

treasure: **Jasmine's Heart**, an enormouse diamond shaped like a heart. This precious stone was a gift for Jasmine, his future wife.

"Legend has it that the storm pushed the galleon onto the CORMORANT ROCKS.

The ship went **DOWN**, and its treasure was never seen again!

"Today, there are rumors that the **GHOST** of Marius von Opul still haunts those waters, searching for Jasmine's Heart."

GALLEON

A galleon is a large, three-masted warship. During the fifteenth and sixteenth centuries, this type of ship transported treasures and other cargo.

AT THE OLDE CHEDDAR SHOP

At that very same moment, at the **Olde Cheddar Shop**, the residents of Whale Island had more pressing matters on their minds. They were busy squeaking about new **HYDROFOIL FERRIES**.

Captain Coral

The two oldest families on Whale Island, the **Squids** and the **Whales**, were gossiping about Captain Coral, a **CHARMING** seamouse who'd recently moved to Whale Island. The minute his brand-new **superfast** hydrofoil ferry docked at the port, word got out that he was planning to open a new boating company, **Whale Island Waterways**.

Captain Coral was offering new routes with low prices for his hydrofoil ferry service, to the great *excitement* of the rodents on the island. Previously, anyone who wanted to go to Mouse Island had to go through **Vince Guymouse**, captain and sole owner of **Maritime Mouseportation**. Every mouse on the island liked Vince, but no rodent ever objected to a little friendly **COMPETITION**.

From behind the shop's counter, Oilskin Whale,

Vince Guymouse

also known as Smudge, said, "The new **HYDROFOIL FERRY** is much bigger and more powerful than Vince's. Think of all the tourists it could bring to the island!" Smudge was the owner of the **Olde Cheddar Shop**. He licked his whiskers in anticipation of new customers.

"Captain Coral sure knows a lot about the **sea**!" commented Smudge's brother Leopold, who was a fishermouse.

"He's a very **nice-looking rodent**, too," said Sardinia Squid, who was also a fishermouse. Sardinia's sisters Mary and Lavender nodded in agreement.

From the darkest corner of the room, an unexpected voice **shrilled**, "A big loudsnout! That's what your Captain Coral is! A big loudsnout and nothing more!" It was the voice of Devon Whale, the father of the Whale clan. "He's been on the island just a few days, and already he's sticking his snout into everything. **QUESTIONS, QUESTIONS,** always **QUESTIONS**! I don't like rodents who ask too many questions! Plus, when he SMILES you can't see his teeth. He's hiding something, or I'll be a SEA MONKEY'S uncle."

Meanwhile, at the harbor, a crowd had gathered to ADMIRE the Neptune, Captain Coral's new hydrofoil ferry. The captain *willingly* showed off his beautiful boat. "I'm waiting for my license to transport rodents," he explained. "Until that comes through, I'm just taking trial **RUNS** around the island, learning the best routes to Mouse Island."

Vince Guymouse stood nearby, fuming. "You'll be waiting a while longer for your license if I have anything to squeak about it," he muttered. "**What a sewer rat!**"

SEA TURTLE HATCHLINGS

Back at Mouseford Academy, **Professor van Kraken** was finishing up his lecture. "So every year at Turtle Beach, we are lucky enough to assist in the hatching of the sea turtle eggs. If my calculations are correct, the hatching will take place the day after tomorrow. I invite all interested students to accompany me to Turtle Beach to welcome the new babies. Afterward, we can take a **dip in the water**!"

The thought of helping baby sea turtles make their way to the sea got everyone **excited**. The students broke into applause.

CLAP CLAP CLAP CLAP CLAP CLAP

SEA TURTLES

Female sea turtles lay their eggs in holes they dig on the beach. Usually, they return to the same beach where they were born to lay their eggs. We still don't understand how they find the same spot.

The female sea turtle comes ashore at night and crawls to a place above the high-tide line, digs a body pit with her front flippers, and then digs an egg cavity with her hind flippers. There she lays anywhere between fifty and two hundred eggs. When she's done, she covers the hole with sand and returns to the sea.

The eggs incubate for forty-five to seventy days. Hatchlings use a temporary egg tooth, a caruncle, to help break open the shell. It can take three to seven days for the young turtles to dig their way to the surface. Then, at night, they leave the nest and crawl to the sea.

"What do you say, sisters? Let's go get our underwater EQUIPMENT ready and put it in Pamela's SUV," Violet suggested as she and her friends filed out of the auditorium.

Nicky stared at her in disbelief. "**NOW?!** Violet, the thing with the professor isn't until the day after tomorrow!"

"You're right, but Professor Stilton always says it's good to prepare in advance!" Violet replied.

At that moment, Professor van Kraken walked out of the auditorium. Violet turned so PALE that Pamela was afraid she was going to faint. "**Vi**, are you okay?"

Before Violet could answer, Colette squeaked, "**No, she's not. She has a crush on the professor!**"

A **sigh** is not exactly an answer, but Violet's was so **long** and deep that her friends understood immediately. Violet didn't have a crush . . .

She had a mega-crush!

A no-SHOW

Violet had to wait for a full two days before joining her fellow students at the **beach** to help Professor van Kraken with the hatching sea turtles. But when the time came at last, the professor was **NOWHERE** to be found! The students waited, and waited, and waited, but finally returned to the academy. They were very disappointed.

Violet was more than disappointed, she was worried. "**SOMETHING'S WRONG.** It's not like the professor to just not show up. Something must have happened to him!"

"Violet, I'm tempted to tease you, but I think you might be right," said Colette.

Nicky nodded in agreement. "Professor van Kraken is usually as punctual as a **cat** at feeding time."

"Let's tell Professor de Mousus," said Pam.

The headmaster didn't seem particularly **worried**. He dialed the number for Tide House, but there was no answer.

"I'm sure there's nothing to **worry** about,"

RING! RING! RING!

the headmaster told the mouselings. "The professor is probably wandering around the island's _seabeds_, lost in the wonders of scientific discovery. Ever since he got a deep submergence vehicle (**DSV***) for his research, he practically lives **underwater**!"

Colette, Pamela, and Nicky nodded. But Paulina took one look at Violet's **worried** snout and piped up, "Professor, would you mind if we went down to **TIDE HOUSE** to check on him?"

Violet smiled gratefully at her friend. The headmaster beamed at them. "Ah, you mouselings are such good citizens!" he said proudly. "Always looking out for others. Of course you may go."

The five mouselings *thanked* the professor and **HEADED STRAIGHT** for the marine biology lab.

*A DSV is a small submarine used by scientists for marine research.

TIDE HOUSE IS DESERTED!

The five mouselings hopped back into Pam's SUV and headed to Tide House. It sat in a *lovely* natural harbor, **BUTTERFLY BAY**. The place was secluded, protected by NIGHTINGALE WOODS on one side and by the sea on the other.

"What a *gorgeous* spot!" Nicky exclaimed.

"Look!" said Pam. "There's Professor van Kraken's car."

CORMORANT ROCKS

TIDE HOUSE

BUTTERFLY BAY

Paulina nodded. "Maybe he's been **HERE** the whole time."

The **Thea Sisters** rang the bell for a long time, but no one answered.

"Maybe the headmaster was right!" Pam said. "The professor must have gone underwater in his **DSV**." She pointed to the **dock**, which stood empty.

"Do you hear that?" Violet asked suddenly. A strange **noise** was coming from the window. "It sounds like an **alarm**! The professor could be in serious trouble. We should go in and check."

"But we can't just knock down the door," Colette objected.

"Look!" Paulina said. "There's an open window."

"I don't know if we should go into the **LAB** without permission," said Pamela.

"On the other paw, we can't leave without making sure the professor is all right."

"Leave it to me, sisters," said Nicky. She SCRAMBLED right up the wall and climbed through the window. The rest of the mouselings watched her in awe.

"Holey cheese, you couldn't pay me to do that," squeaked Colette.

A moment later, Nicky opened the front door. "There's NO ONE here," she said. "But all the computers and lab equipment are on."

Paulina, Violet, Colette, and Pamela followed her in and began LOOKING around. What had happened to Professor van Kraken?

A STRANGE CODE

The lab was in **semidarkness**. Shades were drawn to protect the ultrasensitive equipment from the light of the Sun. Air-conditioning kept the temperature nice and **cool**.

There was a soft buzzing sound, and red and green lights were blinking, indicating that the **computers** were working. One green light drew the mouselings' attention. It was a line moving rapidly **UP** and **down**.

Suddenly, a low whistle came from the loudsqueaker, and the green line went crazy!

TI-TI-TI TA-TA-TA TI-TI-TI

"**What's that?**" asked Pamela, covering her ears.

"It must be the **song of the whales**!" exclaimed Nicky. "We learned about it in marine biology class. That's how whales communicate **underwater**. I think this computer is connected to the bottom of the ocean!"

Pamela twisted her ear. "They're just a little **OUT OF TUNE**!"

"Wait a minute," Paulina interrupted. She was gazing at the line on the computer

screen. "This noise is not **natural**. The rhythm is too regular! It can't be a whale. **SOMETHING ELSE** is making the sounds!"

Colette's fur turned as **white** as mozzarella. "Maybe it's the ghost Professor van Kraken was telling us about! The ghost of Marius von Opul!"

Nicky looked at her doubtfully. Before she could answer, Violet cried out. "Look! Here's something else!" She picked up a long spool of paper that was coming out of the printer under the table.

A **JAGGED** black line ran across the whole strip of paper. It was identical to the green line going across the screen. Violet ran the printout through her **PAWS**. "Paulina's right! It's way too regular! It seems almost like ... **BUT OF COURSE**! It's a signal! It repeats the same pattern over and over!"

"Do you think it's *Morse code*?" asked Pamela.

Nicky took a piece of paper and a *pen* and wrote down the pattern. "It seems to be made up of dots and lines! Dot, dot, dot. Line, line, line. Dot, dot, dot."

"Any idea what it means?" asked Violet.

Nicky nodded. "Three dots correspond with the letter *S*. Three lines with the letter *O* . . ."

Violet understood immediately. "**SOS!** This is a cry for **HELP!**"

CLUE!

Colette's eyes widened. "You mean someone is intentionally transmitting these sounds from the bottom of the ocean?"

Violet nodded. "And there's only one rodent it could be!"

"The ghost of Marius von Opul!" cried Colette.

"Professor van Kraken!" said Paulina at the same time.

Nicky, Pam, and Violet gave Colette a funny look. She looked embarrassed. "Oh — Paulina's right. It must be Professor van Kraken!"

LET'S EVALUATE THE SITUATION:

Professor van Kraken has mysteriously disappeared.

Someone is sending SOS messages in Morse code!

Could it be Professor van Kraken? Or is it the ghost of Marius von Opul?

MORSE CODE

A .−	I ..	R .−.
B −...	J .−−−	S ...
C −.−.	K −.−	T −
D −..	L .−..	U ..−
E .	M −−	V ...−
F ..−.	N −.	W .−−
G −−.	O −−−	X −..−
H	P .−−.	Y −.−−
	Q −−.−	Z −−..

SAMUEL F. B. MORSE (1791-1872)

Samuel Morse developed and built the first American telegraph and created the special code that bears his name in the 1840s. Morse code allows people to translate numbers and letters of the alphabet into sequences of short and long sounds or spaced dots and dashes. The system quickly spread throughout the world as a way to send messages by audible or visual signals. It was an important means of communication for the military until 1999, when it was replaced by newer technologies. Today Morse code is used mostly for fun, though most pilots and ship captains still understand it.

SOS

SOS is an internationally recognized call for help. It is a very easy message to convey in Morse code: three dots, three dashes, and three dots (or · · · — — — · · ·). The letters SOS can stand for "Save Our Ship" or "Save Our Souls."

WINDY GROTTO

"Sssshhhh!" Pamela whispered, pointing to Paulina. "Don't disturb her. I think she's on to something."

Paulina was **scampering** from one computer to the next, squeaking to herself. Her friends didn't understand what she was doing, but they could tell *she* knew what she was doing.

"I'VE GOT IT!" exclaimed Paulina triumphantly. "I've figured out where the signal's coming from!"

On the biggest computer screen was a map of the

western coast of **Whale Island**. A red dot was blinking, revealing the source of the signal.

"WINDY GROTTO!" said Paulina.

CLUE!

Violet scurried out of the laboratory as if she were

WINDY GROTTO

The mysterious call for help is coming from Windy Grotto!

running the last hundred yards at the New Mouse City marathon. The other mouselings looked at one another, then followed her.

Once they got outside, the mouselings **CLAMBERED** into Pamela's **SUV**. The shortest **ROAD** to **WINDY GROTTO** was an **old** path that cut through the woods. When they reached the coast, they had to leave the car and **scamper** down a **STAIRCASE** carved out of **rock**.

They reached a tiny beach and looked around in confusion.

"Where did all the **SAND** go?" asked Nicky.

"And where's the entrance to the cave?" Colette added, **bewildered**.

"It's **high tide**," explained Paulina. "When we came here last month, it was low tide, so the beach was a lot bigger. Now is the time when the tide is at its highest, so the water has covered the entrance to the cave."

"So that means . . ." Pam said slowly.

Paulina nodded. "If we want to go in, we need to go underwater!"

"Uh-oh," said Nicky. She was not at all **ENTHUSIASTIC** about the idea. She suffered from **CLAUSTROPHOBIA** — she couldn't stand being in tight spaces, and that included going underwater.

But Professor van Kraken was **trapped** in Windy Grotto, and he'd been sending those strange **SOS** signals. He needed help fast! There was only one thing to do.

SCUBA DIVING!

The **Thea Sisters** went back to the SUV to get their underwater equipment. Then they put on their wet suits and jumped into the water. Pamela led the **WAY**. She had often gone diving in Windy Grotto and knew it like the back of her paw.

She swam confidently through the opening in the cave, glancing over her shoulder occasionally to make sure her friends were following.

At the Bottom of the Ocean!

WHALES SING . . .

HUMPBACK WHALE
AND BLUE WHALE

Whales emit a series of sounds to communicate with one another. Some species of whales produce sounds that vaguely resemble human sounds. Two groups in particular, the humpback whale and the blue whale, are known for their "singing." Male whales sing only during mating season, but scientists aren't sure if this is part of their courtship ritual.

. . . AND THE SHRIMP PLAY CASTANETS!

CLAP
SNAP

Some of the first sounds that were recorded from the bottom of the sea were those produced by snapping shrimp. These crustaceans produce clicks by snapping their pincers shut. The sound is so loud that submarines have used it to escape detection by enemy sonar.

ECHOLOCATION

Sound is very important both for communication and for orientation underwater. The denser the water, the faster and easier sound travels. Whales, dolphins, and porpoises all use sound to communicate. Using echolocation, toothed dolphins and killer whales are able to assess the speed, size, and shape of objects and sea life hundreds of yards away. They send out clicks that travel rapidly through the water, then bounce back at the dolphin or whale, revealing information about what lies ahead.

At first, the mouselings couldn't see anything because of the darkness inside the cave. So Pam reached for her **FLASHLIGHT**.

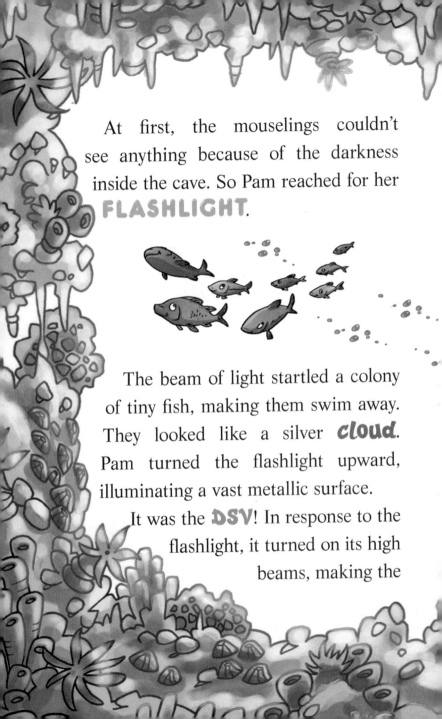

The beam of light startled a colony of tiny fish, making them swim away. They looked like a silver **cloud**. Pam turned the flashlight upward, illuminating a vast metallic surface.

It was the **DSV**! In response to the flashlight, it turned on its high beams, making the

water and the cave walls SHIMMER.
The mouselings **SQUINTED**. All
around them, the walls were covered
with coral and brightly colored sponges.
The Thea Sisters were squeakless
with wonder. It was one of the most
FABUMOUSE sights they'd ever seen!

Suddenly, the DSV's engine started up.
Colette, Nicky, Pam, Paulina, and Violet
swam toward it. As they drew closer,
they noticed it looked a little
banged up.

Violet pressed her snout up to a porthole. Inside she saw **PROFESSOR VAN KRAKEN**!

He SMILED hopefully and waved hello with his **PAW**.

A MATTER OF PERMITS

Meanwhile, back on **Whale Island**, **Vince Guymouse** was in the Coast Guard office, demanding answers.

Who was Captain Coral? Where had he come from? How could he have gotten permission to open a new **boating** company so quickly?

Assistant Chief Seadog

CLUE!

"SALTY CHEESE RINDS, I've been trying for a whole year to get permission to expand my company!" Vince Guymouse BARKED. "Then along comes this Coral rat and steals my job just like that?!"

Chief Seadog stared at him *calmly*. "Don't get your tail in a twist, Vince. I don't have anything to do with it! Call the **MAIN OFFICE** in New Mouse City. They give the permits. I just make sure that the paperwork is in order once it hits my desk."

"Well then, MAKE SURE!" screeched Vince.

Chief Seadog hardly noticed. He was too busy thinking about the boat ride he was going to take on the Neptune after lunch.

It's strange that Captain Coral got his permits so easily.

THEA SISTERS
TO THE RESCUE!

Back in **Windy Grotto**, Colette, Nicky, Pam, Paulina, and Violet were determined to get to Professor van Kraken. Violet was the first to come out of the water and climb onto the **DSV**. She **scampered** all the way to the emergency hatch.

Colette and Paulina followed her, while Pamela and Nicky **swam** around it, checking for damage. There were only dents and **scratches** along the sides. The mouselings were puzzled. Why hadn't the professor come out of the cave?

Pamela found the answer: A **GIANT** rock had gotten stuck between the **DSV**'s propeller and its

PROTECTIVE GRATE, stopping it from spinning. Pam and Nicky carefully tried to dislodge it.

Meanwhile, Violet tried with all her might to open the access hatch, but it was **blocked**, too!

She was **frustrated**, but then she remembered what her **GRANDPA CHEN** used to say: where two paws fail, four can succeed! And there were Paulina and Colette right behind her, ready to help.

GRANDPA CHEN: Where two paws fail, four can succeed!

Even six paws didn't do the trick. This was a task for eight **PAWS**: six that pulled from outside (Violet's, Colette's, and Paulina's) and two that pushed from inside (**PROFESSOR VAN KRAKEN'S**).

The hatch suddenly gave way, and the three mouselings almost toppled over the side!

"How are you, Professor?" Violet asked anxiously.

"I've seen better days," he replied, poking his snout out of the **DSV**. He looked a bit **BRUISED**. "But now that you mouselings are here, I feel like I've discovered the chemical compound of blue cheese! How did you find me?

"We heard your **signal**," explained Paulina.

Professor van Kraken SMILED. "So you figured it out! Thank goodness, you realized I was the one sending those signals. I had no idea if anyone would hear me."

"Why don't you tell us what happened, **PROFESSOR VAN KRAKEN**?" Colette interrupted.

"Yes, yes, of course," the professor said. "Well, I always go out early with the **DSV** and explore the **sea** around the **CORMORANT ROCKS**. I follow the whale movements in this part of the bay before checking on the sea turtle eggs at **Turtle Beach**. Then one day, when I was going underwater, I noticed a shipwreck near the rocks!"

"The Queen Mousy!" Violet exclaimed. "You told us about it during your lecture."

"That's right, Violet!" said the professor. "This was big news, but I decided not to reveal it to anyone."

Colette couldn't contain herself. "Jumping tuna fish, why not?" she asked. "An announcement like that would have attracted attention from all around the world!"

"Exactly!" replied the professor, nodding. "That's exactly what I was afraid of. That wreck at the bottom of the ocean has become home to many species of PLANTS and sea creatures. Salvaging it would mean DESTROYING entire colonies of fish. So I decided that before revealing my discovery, I should figure out a way to retrieve the treasure without doing any harm to the environment. Then, once I'd pawed the treasure over to the port authorities, there would be no damage to the ocean life because no one would care about the shipwreck anymore."

"Good plan!" Nicky said approvingly.

"Thank you, Nicky," said PROFESSOR VAN KRAKEN. "Unfortunately, before I could put my plan into action, someone else

discovered the ship! When I arrived this morning, a **FISHING BOAT** was scraping the bottom of the **sea** with a hydraulic dredger! The rodents on that boat must know about the treasure. I tried to stop them, but they attacked me! I was forced to *FLEE* and hide out in this cave. During my escape, the **DSV** banged against the side of the cave opening, and the propeller was damaged."

"What about you?" said Violet. "You look like you got hurt."

HYDRAULIC DREDGER

A hydraulic dredger is a digging machine that removes sand, gravel, and rubble from the ocean floor. Unfortunately, it has been misused by many shellfish fishermen, which has serious consequences for the ocean floor.

The professor nodded. "Yes, when the **DSV** hit the grotto walls, I hit my snout against the instruments. I'm okay, but I was **TRAPPED**, so I tried sending signals using the whale-o-phone."

"The **whale-o-phone**?" asked Paulina.

"It's an instrument that I invented," the professor explained. "It emits sounds that are similar to whale sounds. I made it in **HOPES** of communicating with the whales!"

Luckily, the **Thea Sisters** had understood his call for help and had arrived in time to save him.

SEA LOOTERS

"It makes me so mad to think that those looters are still **destroying** the ocean floor!" Professor van Kraken said, his squeak **cracking** with exasperation.

"Are you sure they're still there?" asked Paulina.

The professor nodded. "I can hear the **noise** of the dredger with my **EQUIPMENT**. I've been listening for the Coast Guard's motorboat, but no such luck. The only thing I've heard is that **TERRIBLE** machine!"

"That means there's no time to lose! We need to stop them immediately!" cried Paulina. She was ready to **jump back** into the water.

Before she could, Nicky and Pamela popped through the hatch.

"We did it!" exclaimed Pam with satisfaction. "We freed the propeller from the ROCK that was blocking it! Now the DSV should be able to start BACK UP!"

"Amazing!" cried the professor. "You mouselings are **phenomenal**!"

Paulina meant business. "Those treasure hunters better not mess with us!"

"Treasure **hunters**?" Pam repeated. "Am I missing something?

Colette quickly filled them in. Nicky and Pam were **INDIGNANT** when they heard the whole **story**.

"We've got to warn the Coast Guard," said the professor. "But the radio's still broken. And I don't have any scuba equipment."

"But we do," said Violet. "We'll swim you to the surface. You can share our oxygen tanks."

Pam nodded. "Then you can drive my **SUV** to the Coast Guard office at the harbor."

"And we'll stay with the **DSV** and try to distract the **looters** from getting to the **treasure**," said Nicky.

"I'm sure I can steer it to the **CORMORANT ROCKS**," said Pam.

"What will we do once we get there?" asked Colette.

"We'll think of something," said Paulina. "We've got to!"

"Let's do it!" said Violet.

Faster than a catfish with a shark on its tail, Violet and Nicky swam Professor van Kraken up to the surface. Then they hurried back to the **DSV** to put the second part of their plan into *ACTION*.

EVERY MOUSE
FOR HERSELF!

Space was tight in the **DSV**. Colette, Nicky, Pam, Paulina, and Violet had to scrunch themselves in. "If I make myself any smaller, I'll disappear!" Colette joked.

Pamela squeezed herself behind the wheel. "It isn't exactly like driving an SUV, but I'll manage."

Their **exit** wasn't the cleanest: Pamela had some trouble figuring out the cave's dimensions. After a few **pirouettes** and one **U-turn**, she finally steered the **DSV** through the cave's opening.

Once it had **emerged**, the **DSV** ran smoothly, so Pamela pushed the **MOTORS** to the **MAX**. She didn't want the looters

AFTER A FEW PIROUETTES

...AND ONE U-TURN...

...THE EXIT!

to **escape** right under their snouts.

CORMORANT ROCKS appeared on the horizon. Right next to them was the fishing boat!

"Let's go under!" suggested Paulina. "That way we'll catch them by surprise."

"Great idea!" cheered Colette.

"Uh-oh! The DSV isn't responding to commands!" shouted Pamela.

Nicky shot her a look of panic. "You're kidding, right?"

Pamela FRANTICALLY moved her paws from one lever to another. "IT WON'T MOVE! The rudder won't move! All the controls are STUCK!"

She pointed toward the looters' fishing boat, which was growing closer and closer every moment. "We're at *FULL SPEED*, and we're heading right for them!"

Colette, Nicky, and Pam wrapped their paws around the rudder, and together all three mouselings pulled as hard as they could. But it wouldn't budge an inch!

Violet was the only one who remained calm. "Sound the *ALARM* to warn them,

IT WON'T MOVE!

Pam! Then we'll have to jump into the water!"

WOOOO-WOOOO-WOOOO-WOOOOO-WOOOOOOO!!!!!!

The sound of the siren made the cabin vibrate.

Nicky pushed the escape hatch open. One after another, the mouselings leaped into the water. The last one to jump was Pamela. She made it out just in time to see the fishing boat maneuvering to avoid **iMPaCt**. Then she went under.

KERPLANGGGG!

As Colette, Nicky, Pam, Paulina, and Violet swam away, they saw the fishing boat swerve abruptly. Luckily, it didn't **capsize**.

The **DSV**, on the other paw, bounced off the boat and crashed up against the rocks. **KERPLANGGG!**

Pamela breathed a **sigh of relief** when she saw that the fishing boat had sprung a leak, nothing worse. It would be enough to stop the looters without putting them in serious danger.

Suddenly, her fur stood on end: Four figures in **BLACK** wet suits swam through the water. They were headed straight for the **mouselings**!

So the looters weren't all on the boat. Some had been working on the **ocean floor** to try to get the **treasure**!

"Look out, sisters!" cried Pam. "They're coming after us!"

The mouselings swam as quickly as they could, but they hadn't gotten far before the four divers seized them, dragging them underwater once more.

Colette, Nicky, Pamela, Paulina, and Violet fought hard. They squirmed around, trying to slip away from their attackers. But the

looters had **PAWS** as strong as a crab's pincers, and they knew how to move in the water. The water CHURNED around them in a whirlwind of bubbles.

Nicky saw that Violet was in trouble and dove down to help her. Nicky FLUNG herself onto her friend's attacker. Surprised, he let Violet go, and she quickly swam away. Then, turning toward Nicky, he grabbed her oxygen tube and ripped it off.

Nicky had no choice but to swim to the surface. She thought she was in **SERIOUS** trouble, but on the horizon, she spotted Captain Coral's hydrofoil ferry, the Neptune!

What luck!

"We're saved!" cried Nicky. She started waving her paws and screaming,

"HeeeLLLP!!!"

WE'RE SAVED?!

When they saw the hydrofoil ferry, the mouselings' **attackers** slipped away, letting Colette, Nicky, Pam, Paulina, and Violet swim to the boat.

Captain Coral hurriedly helped the girls CLIMB on board.

Violet, Paulina, Colette, Nicky, and Pamela

were trembling from shock and fright. They couldn't believe how lucky they had been to find the Neptune.

"What happened, mouselings?" Captain Coral asked. "How did you get all the way out here?"

Violet began to tell Captain Coral what had happened, but VERY QUICKLY things took a turn . . .

. . . for the worse!

The SUSPICIOUS rodents who had attacked them were climbing on board the ship, too!

"What's going on?" Violet asked as Captain Coral greeted the newcomers.

"I think we fell out of the fondue pot and into the fire!" exclaimed Pamela.

"You mean . . ." Colette began.

". . . the captain is in LEAGUE with these looters!" concluded Paulina.

Captain Coral's SMILE made the mouselings' whiskers quiver with **FEAR**.

"Not exactly, my dears!" said Coral. "I'm not in league with them — I'm their boss!" Then he turned to the four divers, who were removing their wet suits. "Did you find the treasure?"

(LUE!

"Yes, boss!" answered the biggest one. "We got it right before these **BUSYMICE** got to us!"

Captain Coral narrowed his eyes at the five mouselings. "We're in a dangerous situation. We don't want any witnesses. **Tie them up** and gag them, then lock them in the storage cabin. I'll decide what to do with them later. First things first—we need to get out of here!"

That no-good Captain Coral is the boss of the looters on the fishing boat! The hydrofoil ferry is just a cover for his real mission: stealing the *Queen Mousy*'s treasure.

"What about the fishing boat, boss?" asked another henchmouse. "It sprang a leak, and it's stuck until we can fix it."

"**Sink it!**" responded Coral. "Now that we've got the treasure, we don't need it anymore!"

The henchmice hustled the **Thea Sisters** into the storage cabin. Then they tied them up, gagged them, and locked them in.

The mouselings exchanged looks of frustration. What next?

Violet **SCANNED** the crowded cabin, desperately searching for something they could use to free themselves. There were life preservers, ropes, cans, fishing hooks, broken lanterns — nothing of any use. Until her eyes fell on a piece of **JAGGED** wood. It would be perfect for cutting **rope**!

FALSE HOPE

The hydrofoil ferry was **_SPEEDING_** toward Mussel Point.

Suddenly, a Coast Guard motorboat pulled up alongside. "**STOP!**"

Chief Seadog's voice **ECHOED** over the squeakerphone. It was so loud, it even reached the ears of the five **Thea Sisters**.

Was help here at last?

"What's wrong, Chief Seadog?" Captain Coral asked CHEERFULLY, stopping a few feet from the motorboat. "Was I going too FAST? The Neptune sails so well, sometimes I have a heavy PAW!"

"It's a pleasure to see your hydrofoil ferry WHIZZ by, Captain Coral!" answered Seadog, climbing onboard the Neptune. "I just have to do a quick check. Sorry for the inconvenience."

Captain Coral smiled good-naturedly. "Do you want to see my documents?" he asked the captain in a friendly tone. "Go right ahead!"

Meanwhile, Colette, Nicky, Pamela, Paulina, and Violet had heard the patrol boat stop and someone SCAMPER on board.

The Thea Sisters couldn't waste any time.

THEY HAD TO ACT FAST!

Violet nodded at her friends. Then she started rubbing the rope up against the **JAGGED** wood.

SALTY SEA URCHINS!

Finally, the rope gave out! With free paws, Violet ripped off her gag and screamed: "HEELLP!!!"

Nobody seemed to hear her.

She looked outside the cabin's only **porthole** and saw Chief Seadog climbing back onto the patrol boat. What could she do? How could she get his attention?

She pushed open the porthole and shouted, "HEELLP!!! HEELLP!!!"

But the rumble of the patrol boat's motor drowned out her squeak.

Violet looked at her friends in desperation. She scurried over and untied them. As she undid Nicky's binds, some writing on a nearby chest got her attention: **FLARES**.

FLARES

All boats must carry safety equipment, including life preservers, fire extinguishers, and flares. These last items explode in the air and give off an intense light that can be seen from far away. They are only used in case of an **emergency**.

Of course! The patrol boat couldn't ignore a help signal!

Chief Seadog spotted the flare in the sky. *What happened to the hydrofoil?* he thought. Something wasn't right!

He turned **BACK**. As his patrol boat drew closer to the **HYDROFOIL FERRY**, he saw a snout poke out of the side **porthole**. It was Violet.

"Crispy squid tentacles!" exclaimed Seadog. "The Neptune's not allowed to carry passengers yet!"

As the motorboat got closer, he could hear Violet's cries for help.

"Salty sea urchins!" he shouted. "That mouseling is calling for **HeLP!**"

BOOOOOOOOOOMMMMM

WE'RE SAVED (FOR REAL)!

Meanwhile, back in the service cabin, the **Thea Sisters** were **struggling** with Captain Coral's henchmice.

Just as Chief Seadog was asking Coral to explain himself, the squeaks of the five girls reached his ears: "**HEELLP! HEELLP! HEELLP!**"

"**SLIMY SEA ANEMONES!**" the chief burst out. "What is going on down there, Coral?!"

He didn't wait for Captain Coral's answer. He ordered his officers to keep an **EYE** on the captain while he went belowdecks.

Captain Seadog burst into the storage cabin. Realizing they'd been caught in

the act, Coral's henchmice surrendered. The mouselings were saved!

In the meantime, **PROFESSOR VAN KRAKEN** had reached town and sounded the alarm. Soon the sea between the port and Mussel Point was filled with patrol boats searching for the **Thea Sisters**! It would have been impossible to get away, even for a superfast boat like the Neptune.

Captain Coral was forced to give up the treasure of the Queen Mousy: a chest filled with jewels and . . . the famous **Jasmine's Heart**!

As Chief Seadog opened the treasure chest, Colette, Nicky, Pam, Paulina, and Violet gazed at the enormouse jewel in awe.

"Flying fish sticks, that has got to be the most amazing thing I've ever seen," breathed Colette.

"Thanks to the **Thea Sisters**, it's safe!" said the chief.

News of the Queen Mousy's discovery and of the mouselings' doings spread across Whale Island faster than the smell of **melting cheese**. By the time Chief Seadog's patrol boat pulled into harbor, a crowd had gathered to meet it. Violet, Nicky, Pamela, Paulina, and Colette were GREETED as heroes, and everyone was eager to see the **treasure**!

An invitation

When the mouselings returned to Whale Island, there was a serious discussion about the future of the treasure. Captain Seadog, Professor van Kraken, and the headmaster decided that it would remain on display in Mouseford Academy's Trophy Room.

After all that *excitement*, Colette, Nicky, Pamela, Paulina, and Violet were ready to settle back into their studies. But it seemed they were destined never to have a moment's *peace* and *quiet*!

A few days later, Violet burst into the room she shared with her friends. "You'll never believe this, sisters! My dad is conducting an **OPERA** in a new theater, and my mom is the star. They've invited us to come to Beijing after our exams to see it!"

"All of us?!" Colette, Paulina, Nicky and Pamela asked in unison.

"Yes, all of us!" Violet confirmed. "There's more. Along with the e-mail from my parents, there was a note from my old friend Xiao. He has a problem and he needs our help."

"Our help?" asked Pam in surprise. "Really?"

Violet turned to Pam. "Last time I was home, I told Xiao how we solved the DRAGON'S CODE," she said. "Now he says we're the only ones who can help his family. I just can't let down an old friend like Xiao. And here's the most interesting part . . . it has to do with a treasure!"

"Another treasure?" Colette asked.

"Treasure hunting is getting to be our specialty!" exclaimed Nicky.

"Beijing!" said Paulina, who loved traveling. "I can't wait!"

SEE YOU LATER, MOUSEFORD!

And so, a few weeks later, Colette, Nicky, Pamela, PAULINA, and **Violet** left MOUSEFORD ACADEMY again.

Exams were finally over, and the **Thea Sisters** thought they'd done well. They bid a fond farewell to all their friends and

BYE!

HAVE A NICE SUMMER!

professors, and promised to keep in touch over the summer.

The five mouselings took a ride on Vince Guymouse's boat to get to Mouse Island, and from there they caught a direct flight to Beijing.

By this time, the mouselings were expert intercontinental travelers. They knew the best way to pass the time on the long, twelve-hour flight was to **relax** and try to sleep. So they all **curled up** their tails and closed their eyes.

Everyone, that is, except Violet. She was too **EXCITED** about showing her friends around her home country. Plus, she was incredibly curious about the **MYSTERY** Xiao had mentioned in his e-mail.

So when they got off the plane in Beijing, Violet could hardly stand up, she was so **tired**! But it didn't **MATTER**. She was home!

CHINA

Official Name: The People's Republic of China
Capital: Beijing
Principal Mountains: Everest, 29,028 feet; K2, 28,250 feet; Kangchenjunga, 28,169 feet; Lhotse, 27,923 feet; Makalu, 27,824 feet — the five highest mountains in the world!
Languages: Mandarin Chinese (official spoken language), and many other regional dialects, plus non-Chinese languages (such as Mongolian, Tibetan, and Uyghur).

BEIJING

Beijing is the capital of the People's Republic of China. The city has a population of around 17.4 million, making it the second most populous city in the country, after Shanghai, which has 18.9 million inhabitants.

Beijing has a very rich history indeed. It became the imperial capital during the Mongol Yuan dynasty (1279–1368). The heart of Beijing, known as the Forbidden City, was once home of the emperors.

THE FORBIDDEN CITY

Between 1407 and 1420, the third emperor of the Ming dynasty built his residence in the center of Beijing. This was no ordinary palace, but an entire city that spread over three square miles. The Imperial Palace and its reception halls, pavilions, offices, and gardens became known as "The Forbidden City," because only the emperor and his chosen family members, and servants were allowed to enter.

Since 1949, visitors have been welcome in the Forbidden City. The city contains 800 buildings with gleaming yellow roof tiles and more than 8,000 rooms. Many buildings are now museums displaying priceless scrolls, thrones, paintings, and jewels.

WELCOME TO BEIJING!

When the **Thea Sisters** stepped off the plane, they found a **limousine** waiting for them. The driver was none other than Xiao himself!

"Welcome to Beijing!" he called, waving to them. "Hi, Zi Iuolan!" he said to Violet.

"**XIAO!**" cried Violet. "**YOU'RE A SIGHT FOR SORE EYES!**" The two old friends hugged each other tightly.

Violet quickly introduced Xiao to her friends. He ushered the five mouselings into the car, loaded up the luggage, and drove off confidently through the chaotic city TRAFFIC. Next to the cars and trucks, there were endless bicycles **DARTING** through the traffic.

"What was that Xiao called you?" Colette asked Violet.

"Zi Iuolan," Violet replied. "It's my CHINESE name. It means 'violet.' Grandpa Chen chose it because the day I was born, a violet bloomed in his greenhouse, even though they were out of season."

"That's a beautiful story and a beautiful name," Paulina said. "Zi Iuolan!"

Outside the windows, very tall, **modern skyscrapers** whizzed by.

"Look up there!" cried Nicky, pointing to the top of a glass building. "They're skyscrapers, sure, but they have pagoda roofs!"

"Slimy Swiss cheese, what's that?" asked Colette, her snout plastered to the window. She was pointing at an **ENORMOUSE** glass dome that seemed to emerge from a small lake. It was glinting in the *sunlight*.

"That's the new **NATIONAL CENTER FOR THE PERFORMING ARTS**!" explained Violet.

"*Fabumouse!*" said Pam. "It looks like a gigantic *WATER* bubble!"

"More like a **spaceship**!" Nicky put in.

Xiao slowed down to give the mouselings a better look. "The National Center for the

THE CHINESE LANGUAGE

Chinese is spoken by more than a billion people, or about one-fifth of the world population. There are more than 750 separate Chinese dialects, eight of which are used widely. The official spoken language of the People's Republic of China is Mandarin Chinese.

Although there are strong pronunciation differences from region to region, for centuries the Chinese have shared a single written language. Chinese does not have an alphabet; it is written in ideograms. An ideogram is a symbol that represents the idea of the object that it refers to. To read the newspaper, you need to know between 2,000 and 3,000 characters. To read classical Chinese or Chinese literature, you need to know a lot more — at least 6,000.

The first written Chinese dates back to 1500–900 B.C. These early characters were carved into animal fossils and turtle shells.

tree 木

door 门

fire 火

forest 林

sun 日

moon 月

ARCHITECTURE IN BEIJING

In Beijing, many different architectural styles exist side by side. They range from ancient monuments of the imperial capital to the most up-to-date glass skyscrapers.

天府井

Performing Arts is one of the marvels of world architecture!" he told them. "Violet's parents are there rehearsing right now."

"I can't wait to see them!" said Violet. "But first, let's get to the hotel so we can have something to **eat**."

Pamela nodded. "Vi, you took the words right out of my snout!"

FIVE-STAR HOTEL!

When the five mouselings entered the suite at their HOTEL, they got more excited than a hamster with a brand-new treadmill.

"Jumping gerbil babies!" cried Pamela. "This place is amazing!"

Colette sank into the *red* silk couch and said, "It's absolutely Fabumouse."

Nicky entered the first bedroom and dove onto the bed. "There's even a WATERBED."

Paulina turned to Violet. "An entire suite just for us?! Violet, it's too much!"

"Squeak for yourself!" said Colette. She was BEWITCHED by all that she saw.

At the center of the room, there was an enormouse bucket of *roses*. Violet picked up the card. "It's from my parents, with lots of love."

Suddenly, Nicky felt a little UNCOMFORTABLE

in such a *luxurious* room. "Are you sure we couldn't have stayed at your house?"

"Sure . . . if my house wasn't in Hangzhou, thousands of miles from here," Violet explained. "China is a really **BIG** country!"

Xiao entered the suite with the bellmice who were carrying the luggage. "Okay, my friends. Get some rest, because tomorrow I'm going to take you to the famous Panjiayuan Market. It's a great place to **SIGHTSEE**, and

it's also the place where our mystery begins."

"Can't you tell us about it now?" Violet begged. "We're so CURIOUS!"

Xiao just laughed. "No way! I need my five expert detectives rested and ready for anything!"

"Xiao is right," said Nicky. "The trip was long. I don't know about you rodents, but I can't wait to take a ratnap on this waterbed!"

AT THE PANJIAYUAN MARKET

The next morning, Xiao and the five mouselings made an early start. They ate a quick breakfast of dumplings and tea in the suite, then scurried out to the Panjiayuan Market.

The Panjiayuan market is the **BIGGEST**, most famouse, and most chaotic market in all of Beijing. It's an enormouse stretch of stalls and stands where you can find all kinds of arts and crafts.

Colette, Nicky, Pamela, and Paulina didn't know what to **LOOK** at first. There was so much to see! There was porcelain, furniture, carpets, clothes, **jewelry**, fans, stamps, *PAINTINGS* on rice paper and silk, brushes,

and colored inks. There were STATUES of jade, wood, bronze, iron, and terra-cotta everywhere!

Colette fluttered like a **butterfly** between stands filled with gorgeous silks and cashmere sweaters.

Nicky visited a stall with the latest martial-arts magazines.

Violet and Xiao caught up on **ALL** the news from Hangzhou and had fun being the group's tour guides.

As for Paulina, she had made a very special find. She beckoned for all her friends and Xiao to come into a small booth in the corner of the market. She was clutching a small silk bag in her paws.

"What do you have in there?" Colette asked CURIOUSLY.

"Something that will help us remember

this trip . . . and our **friendship**!" **exclaimed** Paulina. She opened the sack, and five small SPARKLING stones tumbled out. The mouselings *ooh*ed and *aah*ed at the sight of them.

"There's **ONE** for each of us," she explained. "Each one is *beautiful* on its own, but when they're all together, they are even more special! Just like us! The pink quartz is for Colette, the amber is for Nicky, the amethyst is for Violet, the turquoise is for Pam, and the MOONSTONE is for me!"

Nicky hugged her. "Thanks so much, Paulina! They're gorgeous."

Pamela gave her a *kiss* on the cheek. "Yeah, thanks! You're the best!"

Violet was so *MOVED*, she lost her squeak. She gazed at the STONES in wonder.

Then she remembered her other good friend, Xiao, and why they were here — to help!

"Xiao, you still haven't told us why we're here," she said.

"Not that we're not enjoying ourselves," said Colette, who loved to shop.

"Violet's right. We came here to help you," said Paulina. "What can we do?"

Xiao nodded. "Yes, the time has come. I knew your friends would love the MARKET, Violet — that's one reason we're here. But there is another. About a month ago, my mother was shopping here when she found a beautiful LACQUER box. She purchased it at once and brought it home. That evening, Madame Hu came to our house and insisted on buying it from her."

"Madame Hu?" Violet repeated, sounding alarmed.

"Yes," said Xiao. "She is a mysterious and **INTIMIDATING** figure in Beijing," he explained to the other mouselings. "No one knows exactly what sort of business she's involved in, but apparently it's very **DANGEROUS** to get in her way! She has a thousand eyes in the city. Thousands of mice work for her."

"Why would she want the box?" Violet asked. "I'm sure it's *beautiful*, but there are many beautiful lacquer boxes for sale at the Panjiayuan Market."

"I don't know why, but my mother thinks it might have something to do with a **TREASURE**," Xiao said. As he squeaked, he looked over his shoulder to make sure no one was watching them. "I have it here. Take a look."

Violet took it carefully and looked at the design on the cover. "I've seen this image

before. We had a print of the same thing at home. But of course! Now I remember! It's the Jade Princess!"

"The Jade Princess?" asked Pam. "Who's that?"

"The princess from the fairy tale?" asked Xiao.

"Yes, I'm sure of it!" Violet declared.

Xiao smiled at her. "See? I knew you could help me, Violet!"

CHINESE CRAFTSMANSHIP

China has been renowned for centuries for its beautiful crafts.

SILK

Around 2640 B.C., the Chinese discovered the life cycle of the silk worm and how to weave silk. Everyone wanted to wear this shiny, soft, comfortable, but expensive fabric. By the third century B.C., silk fabrics found their way across the sea to Japan and to the West along routes known as "silk roads."

DRAWINGS ON SILK

The Chinese began painting on silk more than two thousand years ago, long before the invention of paper. The most common form was the hanging scroll, both vertical and horizontal. Scrolls were attached to and wrapped around two lacquered wooden cylinders, which kept the cloth tight and allowed it to be easily rolled up and put away. Landscapes, figures, birds, and flowers were popular subjects.

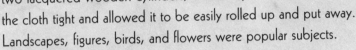

LACQUER OBJECTS

Mainland China has thousands of Asian sumac trees. Their sap has been used for centuries to make a varnish that coats boxes, wagons, boats, musical instruments, and many other precious objects with a glossy and smooth finish. Lacquer is resistant to heat, water, and acid.

A DRAGON-SHAPED
PIN

Xiao had been sure that they were alone. But as he finished squeaking, a jeweled paw with **NAILS** as long as claws grabbed Violet's shoulder.

"What a *beautiful* **LACQUER** box, mouseling! But I'm sorry to tell you that it belongs **TO ME!**"

Violet was stunned. When she turned around, she found a beautiful but **INTIMIDATING** rodent staring at her with eyes of **ICE**. She gasped. It was Madame Hu! Violet had seen pictures of the woman in the newspaper, and

she would have recognized her anywhere.

She was wearing a black silk dress that SHONE like her fur, which was held together by a gold DRAGON-shaped hairpin. A chill ran down Violet's tail.

Before she could squeak, Colette piped up. "I'm sorry, you must be mistaken. This box belongs to **MY FRIEND'S FAMILY**." She took the box out of Violet's paw.

"I will pay you VERY, **VERY** well!" said the mysterious rodent, with a decisive tone that rubbed Colette's fur the wrong way.

"I'm sorry, but it is N O T for sale!" declared Colette.

Suddenly, the friends realized that two of Madame Hu's henchmice were about to grab them! "Paws off, cheddarface!" cried Colette.

CLUE!

Xiao grabbed her by the paw, dragging

her away into the large crowd in a *HURRY.*
Violet, Nicky, Pam, and Paulina scurried
after them.

"**STOP THEM!**" demanded the woman.

"Step on it, mouselings!" yelled Xiao.

Colette, Nicky, Pam, Paulina, and Violet
obeyed without thinking twice. They
squeezed through the narrow passage
between two stands, emerging in a clearing

Why does the box matter so much to the
mysterious rodent?

where JUGGLERS were entertaining a small crowd.

Xiao and the **Thea Sisters** didn't hesitate. They ran into the middle of the show, right through the jugglers' stilts! Thinking the sisters were part of the show, the audience applauded.

Luckily, the two **henchmice** were not as agile: They got tangled up with the stilts and fell down. When they were back on their paws, they tried PUSHING their way through the crowd. But the audience and the jugglers got angry at the interruption and began throwing things at them. Splat! Splat! Splat! The two henchmice were soon covered with eggs, FRUIT, and vegetables!

Quiet as mice, Xiao, Violet, Colette, Nicky, Pamela, and Paulina slipped back to their car and returned to the hotel.

The Thea Sisters entered their suite completely out of breath and very worried.

"That was Madame Hu, right?" asked Nicky. "**HOW DID SHE FIND US?**"

Violet frowned. "Madame Hu is very powerful. She must have decided to have Xiao followed. Then she probably figured she could **steal** the box away from us in the market."

Pam nodded. "It's so busy there, she must have thought no one would notice."

"Why does she want the box so badly?" Paulina asked. "Perhaps Xiao's mother is right about the treasure. And who is this Jade Princess you mentioned?"

"That's a long story," said Violet. "Let me make us some **tea**, to calm us all down, and I'll tell you."

AN ANCIENT
FAIRY TALE

"Once upon a time there lived a very beautiful and very *spoiled* princess," Violet began. "Her name was Yu, which means *jade* in Chinese. She was very proud of her name, and decided she must have the most beautiful and most **precious** jade necklace in the world.

"Merchants from every corner of the empire arrived with *beautiful* stones to show her. But the princess was impossible to please. No jade was beautiful enough for her. She rejected stone after stone and forced the merchants to throw them into the **river**.

"One day, a mouseling dressed in **rags** arrived at the palace. She brought with

her the most perfect jade that any mouse had ever seen. The mouseling said that it was the Jade of Truth. The stone was so extraordinarily smooth, it could have been a mirror. The image that it **reflected** was special: It showed the true snout of anyone who looked into it.

"The princess took the jade and looked into it and saw a lonely, selfish rodent. Five tears fell from her eyes. As they fell, they transformed into five precious stones. The princess gave these stones to the poor mouseling who had revealed her true self.

"From that day on, *Princess Yu* was never the same. She became kind and generous. She didn't think about the most beautiful jade anymore. And she often squeaked of all the beautiful stones that she had rejected, which remained at the bottom of the river."

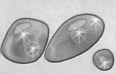

Merchants from every corner of the empire arrived with beautiful jades. But the princess was impossible to please.

Until one day, a young mouseling with the most beautiful stone in the world came to the palace.

The princess looked at her reflection in the jade . . . and saw a lonely, selfish rodent. Five tears fell from her eyes.

From that day on, Princess Yu became kind and generous. And all the beautiful jade stones that she had thrown away remained at the bottom of the river.

THE SECRET OF THE LACQUER BOX

"What a beautiful story!" said Paulina with a sigh. She took the box and opened it. "Moldy mozzarella, there's ANOTHER BOX in here!" she exclaimed. "And ANOTHER! And ANOTHER! And then ANOTHER still!"

Xiao nodded. "Yes, five in all."

"Five boxes, one inside the next," reflected Violet. "Five . . . just like the five tears of the Jade Princess!"

"Five . . . like us!!" said Nicky.

"It's a sign that we're meant to protect this box!" declared Colette.

"We can figure out what it means, I know we can," said Paulina.

"Thank you!" said Xiao. "My mother has

grown very attached to this **LACQUER** box. And she's like you — she doesn't like giving in to **bullies**! But I don't want you to end up in **TROUBLE** because of the box. We must be very careful."

The mouselings agreed. They sat and examined the box for a while longer, each with her own theory about what the box meant. But nothing seemed **RIGHT**.

After an hour or two, Xiao left, and the

Thea Sisters realized that they were really **tired**. It had been a busy day. They decided to order room service and go straight to bed.

Violet was a real sleepysnout. She always needed a good night's sleep. But that night, she kept tossing and turning. She was having the strangest dream.

She dreamed that she was really really small, and the five boxes had become **ENORMOUSE**.

When the boxes were stacked on top of one another, they formed a staircase as tall as a mountain!

In her dream, Violet tried to climb the mountain. Her friends were at the top, and she knew they needed her help. They were being held prisoner by an enormouse **DRAGON** like the one she'd seen on

the pin in Madame Hu's hair!

Suddenly, the **DRAGON** moved and tried to SNAP at her! It was alive!

Violet woke up with a jolt. Her fur was matted with sweat. It was dawn.

Violet scurried into the suite's living room. The five **LACQUER** boxes were still on the table. She looked at them for a long time, then started to put them one on top of the next, just like they had been in her dream.

It seemed like a silly thing to do, but it wasn't! The decorations looked simple, but they lined up perfectly with one another. In fact, when all the five boxes were on top of each other and were turned at the right angle, Violet saw they made a picture: **THE GREAT WALL!**

And there was **more**!

Next to the picture of the wall, Violet

noticed three symbols: 司马台

Just then, Nicky returned from her morning run. She looked at the boxes and asked, "What are you BUILDING there? Do you want to have a cup of **TEA**?"

Yes, Violet definitely needed a cup of tea!

"You have such shadows under your eyes, Violet!" exclaimed Paulina, emerging from her room. "You look more like a **RACCOON** than a mouse! Did you sleep at all last night?"

"I had a funny dream," explained Violet. "The dream gave me an **IDEA**. Look!"

CLUE!

She pointed to the design that ran across the five boxes and added, "This is the Great Wall, and these three symbols mean Simatai!"

The design on the box represents a section the Great Wall of China! Could this be the key to unlocking the secret of the box?

SiMATAi?

The name *Simatai* didn't mean anything to Nicky and Paulina.

"Simatai is a section of the **GREAT WALL**," explained Violet. "It's famouse because it's very beautiful and very **hard** to cross. It's not too far from Beijing, but tourists don't visit it much."

THE GREAT WALL

The Great Wall is a series of walls constructed over two millennia — from the fifth century B.C. until the seventeenth century A.D. The first emperor of a unified China, Qin Shi-huang, linked the walls into a single network in the third century B.C. The wall is estimated to span about 4,000 miles, which is wider than the continental United States!

Some sections of the wall were originally made from packed earth and piled stone. During the Ming Dynasty, brick and mortar made 3,107 miles of the wall 26 feet tall and 30 feet wide at its base. The Great Wall became a UNESCO World Heritage Site in 1987.

"So what you're saying is, these boxes form a sort of **map**!" said Paulina.

At that moment, Pam **CAME OUT** of her bedroom. "Did you say *map*? Every map leads to a **treasure**!"

Violet jumped up. "Crispy cheese rolls! Maybe it's Princess Yu's lost treasure — the jade stones that were thrown into the river!"

Pamela ran to knock at Colette's door. "Wake up, Colette, there's **news**! Violet found the princess's treasure map!"

Her fur disheveled, Colette scampered into the living room. When she saw the boxes

stacked on top of each other, she understood immediately. "So that's why Madame Hu wants it **so badly**!"

"What are we waiting for?" cried Nicky. "It's time for a trip to the Great Wall!"

Immediately, the five mouselings started scurrying around. Suddenly, Paulina stopped. "Wait. What about Xiao?"

Violet shook her snout. "I don't want to get him and his family mixed up in any trouble. He asked for our help, and now we're going to deliver it!"

Nicky nodded in agreement. "We've had lots of **ADVENTURES** together. If anyone knows how get out of a mess, it's us!"

Colette carefully put the lacquer boxes back inside one another. As she did so, she **NOTICED** the insides of the box covers were covered in teeny tiny pictures. "Look!"

The inside of the box had a picture of two LOTUS FLOWERS entwined together.

"The **Fairy Tower**!" Violet cried. "There are many towers along the **GREAT WALL**, but the Fairy Tower is the only one with a decorated **STONE** archway. Just like the lotus flowers on this design!"

"Good work, Vi!" cheered Pam. "Now we know where to start!"

LET'S EVALUATE THE SITUATION!

1. The lacquer box tells the story of the Jade Princess and her lost treasure hidden in the river. *Yes.*

2. The box is hiding a map of the Great Wall. *Yes.*

3. Madame Hu, a sinister stranger, is searching for the box. Is she after the princess's treasure? *Yes!*

AT THE GREAT WALL

Half an hour later, the Thea Sisters hurried out of their hotel. Their DESTINATION: Simatai, on the GREAT WALL. The forecast for the day was splendid: The sky was clear and the sun was shining.

A bus took the *mouselings* to the train station a few miles outside BEIJING.

The **mountains** looked majestic, with the Great Wall an enormouse crown SPARKLING along the crest. Colette, Nicky, Pam, and Paulina gazed at the wall in awe.

"Chewy **cheese crepes**, that has

WHITE CLOUD TOWER

SIMATAI

CABLE CAR

got to be the most gorgeous thing I've ever seen," Colette said with a sigh.

As for Paulina and Pamela, they were squeakless.

Nicky dragged them toward the cable car. **"LET'S GO UP**, quick! I can't wait to see the view from up there!"

The higher the tram went, the more *magnificent* the scenery became around them.

A few minutes later, the mouselings scrambled off the cable car at White Cloud Tower.

"From here, we go by paw," warned Violet. "It's **STEEP!**"

"Hooray!" said Nicky. "I could use a little exercise."

The five mouselings began their hike cheerfully. They chattered away, pointing

out sights to one another. None of them suspected that they were being *followed*!

Since the moment they'd left the market, the MOUSELINGS' every **MOVE** was being closely watched. Xiao had warned them that Madame Hu had a thousand **EYES**. Even now, her spies had kept them close.

One spy had **watched** them leave their hotel. Another had *followed* them to the cable car. A third and final spy had *informed* Madame Hu of their movements and their intentions!

When Madame Hu had *heard* where the five mouselings were **headed**, she realized she no longer needed

One spy had watched them leave their hotel.

the **LACQUER** box. Colette, Nicky, Pam, Paulina, and Violet were bringing her right where she wanted to go: to the *Jade Princess*'s treasure!

Another had followed them to the cable car.

Don't let them out of your sight! I'm coming!

THE FAIRY TOWER

The walk along the section of the wall that led to the **Fairy Tower** was exhausting but exhilarating. The five mouselings had brought drinks and cheese sandwiches with them, and the *beautiful* view made their journey even more delightful.

"Walking along the Great Wall is like walking along a snake's back," said Nicky.

"More like walking along the back of an enormouse sleeping **dragon**!" said Pam.

WHITE CLOUD TOWER

FAIRY TOWER

SIMATAI

CABLE CAR

STAIRWAY TO HEAVEN

SIMATAI VILLAGE

"It's as if we're walking along a CHINESE scroll, and our pawprints are the words that are inscribed on it," said Paulina.

Colette **LOOKED** at her in admiration. "You are a true poet, Paulina!"

The five mouselings **hiked** until they finally reached the Fairy Tower. Their paws were aching from their long trek, but their spirits were SOARING!

The mice sat for a while to

catch their breath. Pamela took the
sandwiches out of her backpack
and shared them with her friends.

Violet looked at the lotus
FLOWeRS etched into the stone archway.
They were exactly the same as the flowers
inside the cover of the lacquer box. She
pulled out the boxes and examined their
covers, hoping to find some new clues.

Inside the second cover was a picture of a
staircase. Where had she seen one like that
before? Violet looked down from the Great
Wall and spotted a very steep staircase that
descended into the WOODS
below. In the guidebook, it
was called the Stairway to
Heaven.

Violet turned to her
friends, who were munching

their sandwiches cheerfully. "Let's go! We need to use that stairway!"

The five mouselings leaped to their paws and carefully made their way DOWN the stairs.

"Look over there!" cried Pam. "There's a small cottage between those trees!"

Violet jumped up. "A cottage! On the third cover there's a picture of the roof of a house!" She gazed at the spot Pam had indicated and noticed a path that led from the wall into the woods.

At that moment, a HELICOPTER flew over them.

CHOP-CHOP-CHOP-CHOP-CHOP-CHOP!

A COTTAGE IN THE WOODS

Colette, Nicky, Pam, Paulina, and Violet didn't know it, but Madame Hu was in that helicopter! The five mouselings kept scampering along until they reached the cottage. Its **stone** walls looked old, but the red tiled roof was new, and there was even a satellite dish.

The **Thea Sisters** looked at one another, unsure what to do next. Finally, Pam took action. She boldly knocked on the door. It was immediately opened by an old rodent. "Hello," she greeted them. "Please come in and make yourselves comfortable! I'm always so happy when I have guests!"

No sooner had the old rodent closed

the door behind them than a push from the outside burst it open again! The old rodent almost TOPPLED OVER. Violet quickly reached out and steadied her with one paw.

Madame Hu appeared at the doorstep, followed by two henchmice. She turned to the five mouselings. "We meet again," she said with a mocking SMILE. Then, LOOKING AROUND, she said, "So this is where the treasure is hidden!"

Violet, Nicky, Pamela, Colette, and Paulina were squeakless. The old rodent, on the other paw, didn't seem surprised. "Ah,

Princess Jade's treasure! So that's the reason for all the visitors! **Good, good!** Then I imagine you have the **LACQUER** box?"

Violet **STARED** at her, astounded. The shock of Madame Hu's **appearance** was nothing compared to what she felt at the old rodent's words.

"Out with the box!" ordered Madame Hu. Her two henchmice **moved** threateningly toward the mouselings.

Violet opened her bag and showed them the box, but she did not take it out.

The old rodent seemed satisfied. "Yes, I recognize it! It is definitely the one. But the last **PIECE** is missing. I possess the last box, the *smallest* one, the one that leads to the treasure!"

As she squeaked, she opened a drawer and took something out. Before the five mouselings could see what it was, one of Madame Hu's henchmice snatched it from the old woman and pawed it to his boss.

"**Mine**, at last!" cackled Madame Hu. "Finally my quest is complete! I have followed the *princess*'s box through all the markets in China. Now, at long last, the treasure is **mine**!"

With that, Madame Hu spun around and scurried out of the cottage, with her henchmice on her paws.

"Come on, let's go!" **CRIED** Pamela. "We've got to find out where they're going!"

Nicky put a paw on her shoulder. "It's **USELESS**! We don't have any proof against those rat burglars."

"Then what next?" asked Colette.

"I don't know," said Paulina sadly. "The trail has gone **COLD**."

A SENSATIONAL
DEVELOPMENT!

Violet turned to the old rodent and helped her sit down. "Are you all right, ma'am?"

A SMILE lit up the old rodent's snout. "Never been better in all my life, child. Now let's get back to our treasure!"

When she noticed the SURPRISE in Violet's eyes, the old rodent seemed amused. "HEE-HEE! You didn't think that I would let that WITCH get away with such a precious treasure, did you? My family has guarded it for generations. I am a descendant of the little mouse who gave

Princess Yu the Jade of Truth!"

Colette, Nicky, Pam, Paulina, and Violet were stunned by this revelation. There was a moment of silence. Then Paulina said, "Then what did you give Madame Hu?"

The old rodent giggled. "Only what she deserved. I will also give you what you deserve — if you can answer the riddle that the princess entrusted to my ancestor, the guardian of the box, so many centuries ago," explained the old woman solemnly. "The riddle is this: What is the name of the most precious stone?"

The five Thea Sisters looked at one another thoughtfully.

"I think the most precious stone is a diamond," mused Colette. "It must be the Millennium Diamond! It's the LARGEST diamond in the world!"

"That can't be the answer to the riddle," said Nicky. "During the *princess*'s time, it hadn't been discovered yet."

Violet agreed. "Plus, jade has always been the most precious stone for the CHINESE people. But I don't think that's the right answer, either."

The five mouselings discussed the riddle at length. They came up with many answers, but none of them seemed **RIGHT**. The old woman rodent seemed to appreciate the effort they were making. She brought them some tea.

Paulina took out the bag with the stones that she had bought for her friends and pawed them to Violet. "For me, the most precious stones in the world are these," she said.

"*YEAH, FOR US, TOO!*" agreed Pam, Nicky, and Colette.

Violet SMILED at her friends. Then she turned to the old rodent and showed her the five small stones. "We don't know the name of the most precious stone. But for us, the stones that are worth the most are these five. They represent our friendship!"

The old rodent looked the mouselings in the EYE one by one. Finally, she squeaked, "Yes, I can tell that you five are bound together by sincere feelings of affection. I can trust you." She paused, then smiled. "There is no other clue to the treasure. I gave Madame Hu a fake clue to throw her OFF TRACK. Princess Yu ordered that her treasure go to someone who was worthy. It needed to be a rodent who was pure of heart, generous, and HONORABLE. She

Friendship!

wanted it to be someone who is able to appreciate the most important thing in life — friendship. Like you five mouselings, who are such close friends. **SO LET'S GO!** I'll show you the way to the **treasure**!"

THE JADE PRINCESS'S TREASURE

The old rodent led them out the back door of her cottage. "Follow this path," she instructed. "It will take you to the river. A little downstream, you will see a forest of weeping willows. Stop when you get there."

Without further ado, the old woman bid the Thea Sisters farewell.

Colette, Nicky, Pam, Paulina, and Violet started down the path. About fifteen minutes later, they reached the river. The sun glinted off the water, and the branches from the weeping willows whispered in the gentle wind. It almost seemed as though the trees were trying to get their attention.

The mouselings pushed past the long branches and discovered a pool of WATER. It was a marvelous natural aquarium, with fish flashing between the water lilies.

"It's enchanting!" breathed Paulina.

"Yes, it is," began Violet. Then she stopped abruptly, for she saw something shining in the middle of the pool. She leaned forward, GAZING at the water.

Colette, Nicky, Pam, and Paulina had noticed it, too. They crowded in close to one another to get a better look.

A mountain of small jade stones SHIMMERED beneath the water's surface! The flow of the river had smoothed the stones over time. Now the sun, reflecting against the water, made them glitter with all the colors of the rainbow!

For a moment, the mouselings were too

stunned to squeak. Then they looked at one another.

"Should we remove the **treasure**?" asked Colette hesitantly. "It seems wrong somehow."

Nicky nodded in agreement. "This is its **place**. It belongs here."

"Yes," said Violet. "This is the place where legends become **REALITY**."

THE JADE OF TRUTH

The sun was starting to **SET**. It was time to **turn back**. Dusk was falling over the woods. Colette, Nicky, Pam, Paulina, and Violet had not imagined they would be out so long.

Violet frowned. "I lost track of time! The **LAST** bus has probably returned to Beijing by now."

"How will we get home?" Colette asked anxiously.

"Let's go back to the **old rodent**," Nicky proposed. "Maybe she knows another way to get back to Beijing."

When the **Thea Sisters** returned to the cottage, they saw **POLICE OFFICERS** taking Madame Hu and her henchmice away in pawcuffs!

Violet **SCAMPERED** up to the old rodent.

"**RANCID RAT HAIRS**, what happened? Are you okay? Did they come back to get **REVENGE**?"

The old woman SMILED. She seemed to be enjoying herself more than ever. "My dear, I am just fine! I knew it was only a matter of time before that evil rodent realized I'd tricked her. So while you and your friends were at the river, I called the police!"

"Good for you!" cheered Pamela.

"What about the treasure?" the old rodent asked. "Did you find it?"

Violet nodded. "Yes. And we left it right where it belongs."

The old rodent beamed at her. Then she opened a drawer and took out a small bundle wrapped in a tissue. She unwrapped it slowly and revealed . . . the Jade of Truth! The one that had belonged to Princess Yu!

Colette, Nicky, Pam, Paulina, and Violet gazed at it in wonder.

"This stone is the true treasure," the old rodent explained. "I have kept it safe my whole life. Now it must pass into your paws, because you have proved your souls are noble. This is what Princess Jade would have wanted!"

A NIGHT AT THE OPERA

The next evening, it was finally time to go to the opera in the new **NATIONAL CENTER FOR THE PERFORMING ARTS**.

Colette, Nicky, Pamela, PAULINA, and **Violet** were practically jumping out of their **fur** with excitement. As they settled into their seats with Xiao, they filled him in on their adventures from the previous day. He was squeakless with *surprise* and awe.

"Now I know I did the right thing when I asked you for help, Vi," said Xiao. Violet blushed.

Colette pulled the lacquer boxes out of her pawbag. "Here, Xiao. We brought these back

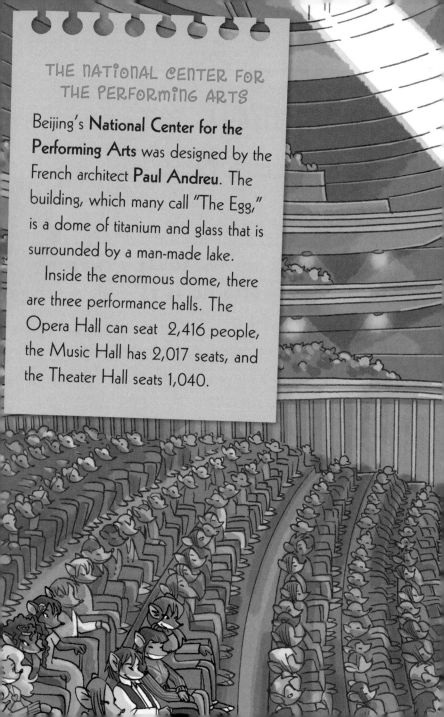

THE NATIONAL CENTER FOR THE PERFORMING ARTS

Beijing's **National Center for the Performing Arts** was designed by the French architect **Paul Andreu**. The building, which many call "The Egg," is a dome of titanium and glass that is surrounded by a man-made lake.

Inside the enormous dome, there are three performance halls. The Opera Hall can seat 2,416 people, the Music Hall has 2,017 seats, and the Theater Hall seats 1,040.

safe and sound. We knew your mother would want them back."

Xiao smiled. "Thanks, Colette. I think she'll like the **story** I have for her even better than the boxes!"

"Shhhh!" Nicky hissed. "The opera is beginning!"

The five mouselings and Xiao fell silent as the curtain went up. Violet's heart swelled with pride when she saw *her mother* onstage. She looked at her friends and realized how L U C K Y she was to have such wonderful rodents in her life.

As for me, I had never left my mouse hole in New Mouse City. But as Colette, Nicky, Pam, Paulina, and Violet finished telling their tale, I felt as if I'd been all the way to China! I could hardly believe all the *twists* and *turns* of their *incredible* adventure.

"What an amazing journey!" I squeaked as I looked through some photos from their trip. "You five mouselings have really become amazing investigators. I'm so proud."

"There's one last thing we have to show you," said Violet shyly.

"It's a surprise for you," Nicky put in.

Pam pawed me a beautiful lacquer box. Carefully, I opened it. Inside there was a stone wrapped in a silk cloth. It was a *splendid* jade, shiny like a mirror. I saw my **reflection** on its surface. It was the Jade of Truth!

There was a note attached to it. "For Thea, the keeper of our **friendship**! Love, *Pamela*, *Nicky*, *Colette*, PAULINA, and **Violet**."

They were more than friends. They were sisters!

THEA SISTERS

Want to read the next adventure
of the Thea Sisters?
I can't wait to tell you all about it!

THEA STILTON AND THE SECRET CITY

The Thea Sisters head to Peru, where a good friend of Paulina's is in danger. There, the five mice climb the Andes Mountains in search of a mysterious treasure that's hidden in the Secret City of the Incas. It's an adventure to remember!

And don't miss any of my other fabumouse adventures!

THEA STILTON AND THE DRAGON'S CODE

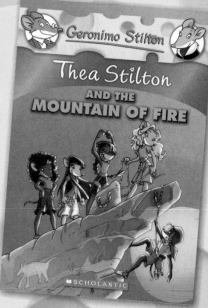

THEA STILTON AND THE MOUNTAIN OF FIRE

Want to read my next adventure?
I can't wait to tell you all about it!

MIGHTY MOUNT KILIMANJARO

Rat-munching rattlesnakes! I can't believe it. I just let my super-sporty friend Bruce Hyena convince me to go on another one of his extreme adventures. You know me . . . I just can't say no to a friend! This time, we're going to be climbing to the top of the famouse Mount Kilimanjaro in Africa. Moldy mozzarella! I'm in no shape for a mountain climb. How will I ever make it to the top?

And don't miss any of my other fabumouse adventures!

#1 LOST TREASURE OF THE EMERALD EYE

#2 THE CURSE OF THE CHEESE PYRAMID

#3 CAT AND MOUSE IN A HAUNTED HOUSE

#4 I'M TOO FOND OF MY FUR!

#5 FOUR MICE DEEP IN THE JUNGLE

#6 PAWS OFF, CHEDDARFACE!

#7 RED PIZZAS FOR A BLUE COUNT

#8 ATTACK OF THE BANDIT CATS

#9 A FABUMOUSE VACATION FOR GERONIMO

#10 ALL BECAUSE OF A CUP OF COFFEE

#11 IT'S HALLOWEEN, YOU 'FRAIDY MOUSE!

#12 MERRY CHRISTMAS, GERONIMO!

#13 THE PHANTOM OF THE SUBWAY

#14 THE TEMPLE OF THE RUBY OF FIRE

#15 THE MONA
MOUSA CODE

#16 A CHEESE-
COLORED CAMPER

#17 WATCH
YOUR WHISKERS,
STILTON!

#18 SHIPWRECK ON
THE PIRATE ISLANDS

#19 MY NAME
IS STILTON,
GERONIMO STILTON

#20 SURF'S UP,
GERONIMO!

#21 THE WILD,
WILD WEST

#22 THE SECRET
OF CACKLEFUR
CASTLE

A CHRISTMAS
TALE

#23 VALENTINE'S
DAY DISASTER

#24 FIELD TRIP TO
NIAGARA FALLS

#25 THE SEARCH
FOR SUNKEN
TREASURE

#26 THE MUMMY
WITH NO NAME

#27 THE CHRISTMAS
TOY FACTORY

#28 WEDDING
CRASHER

#29 DOWN AND OUT
DOWN UNDER

#30 THE MOUSE ISLAND MARATHON

#31 THE MYSTERIOUS CHEESE THIEF

CHRISTMAS CATASTROPHE

#32 VALLEY OF THE GIANT SKELETONS

#33 GERONIMO AND THE GOLD MEDAL MYSTERY

#34 GERONIMO STILTON, SECRET AGENT

#35 A VERY MERRY CHRISTMAS

#36 GERONIMO'S VALENTINE

#37 THE RACE ACROSS AMERICA

#38 A FABUMOUSE SCHOOL ADVENTURE

#39 SINGING SENSATION

#40 THE KARATE MOUSE

And don't forget to look for

#41 MIGHTY MOUNT KILIMANJARO

MOUSEFORD
TEACHERS' LIVING QUARTERS
ATHLETIC FIELDS
DORMS
GARDEN
SOUTH TOWER
LIBRARY

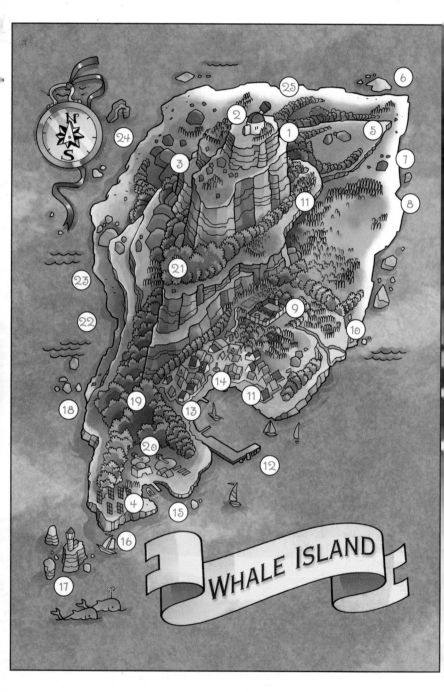

MAP OF WHALE ISLAND

1. Falcon Peak
2. Observatory
3. Mount Landslide
4. Solar Energy Plant
5. Ram Plain
6. Very Windy Point
7. Turtle Beach
8. Beachy Beach
9. Mouseford Academy
10. Kneecap River
11. Mariner's Inn
12. Port
13. Squid House
14. Town Square
15. Butterfly Bay
16. Mussel Point
17. Lighthouse Cliff
18. Pelican Cliff
19. Nightingale Woods
20. Marine Biology Lab
21. Hawk Woods
22. Windy Grotto
23. Seal Grotto
24. Seagulls Bay
25. Seashell Beach

THANKS FOR READING, AND GOOD-BYE UNTIL OUR NEXT ADVENTURE!

THEA SISTERS